For my BSF—Best Stephen Forever—I love you.
—TSS

This book is dedicated with love to Desmond
and Jude: a couple of stinkers!
—SKS (the Funky Uncle)

Punk Skunks
Text copyright © 2016 by Trisha Speed Shaskan
Illustrations copyright © 2016 by Stephen Shaskan
All rights reserved. Manufactured in China.
No part of this book may be used or reproduced in any manner whatsoever
without written permission except in the case of brief quotations embodied
in critical articles and reviews. For information address HarperCollins Children's Books,
a division of HarperCollins Publishers, 195 Broadway, New York, NY 10007.
www.harpercollinschildrens.com
ISBN 978-0-06-236396-1

The artist used Photoshop to create the digital illustrations for this book.
Typography by Rachel Zegar
15   16   17   18   19   SCP   10   9   8   7   6   5   4   3   2   1
❖
First Edition

PUNK SKUNKS

Written by **Trisha Speed Shaskan**

Illustrated by **Stephen Shaskan**

WITHDRAWN

HARPER
An Imprint of HarperCollinsPublishers

Kit and Buzz were BSFs—

best skunks forever. Each day, Kit
banged on Buzz's door.

Together, they zoomed through the Burrows.

Kit skateboarded.

RATTLE.

CLATTER.

SMACK!

SMACK!

Buzz biked.

CLICKETY.

CLACK.

BUMP!

BUMP!

"DIG IT!" Kit said.
"Rock on," Buzz said.

Kit and Buzz played at the park.

Buzz painted.

SWOOSH.
WHOOSH.
SPLAT!
SPLAT!

Kit hopscotched.

SLAP!
WHAP!
THUMP!
THUMP!

"**DIG IT!**" Kit said.
"Rock on," Buzz said.

Buzz strummed.

WAHH!

WAHH!

REN!

REN!

Together, they sang,

"WE'RE BUZZ AND KIT.
THIS IS OUR SONG.
WE BOTH DIG IT.
AND WE ROCK ON."

One day while rocking out, Kit said,
"I wanna sing a new song about skating."
"No way," Buzz said. "I wanna sing a
new song about painting."

"Skating," Kit said.

"Painting," Buzz said.

Rattle. Clatter.
Kit drummed!

Swoosh. Whoosh.
Buzz strummed!

Kit exploded.

Buzz imploded.

"You STINK!" they yelled, which is
the one phrase the BSFs had never said
to each other before.

The next day, Kit didn't bang on Buzz's door.

They didn't zoom through the Burrows

or play at the park.

And worst of all:

They didn't rock out.

Kit crash, bam, boomed.
But she didn't dig it.

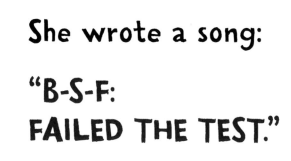

She wrote a song:

"B-S-F:
FAILED THE TEST."

She hummed and drummed.
But it was all wrong.

"I give up," she said.
Kit set out to sell her drums.

Meanwhile, Buzz *ren, ren, renned*. But he didn't rock on.

He wrote a song:

"B-S-F:
WHAT A PEST."

He hummed and strummed.
But it was all wrong.

At the music shop, Kit was surprised to see Buzz.
"Wanna write a new song?" Buzz asked.

"Together?" Kit said.

Kit and Buzz wrote

and rewrote

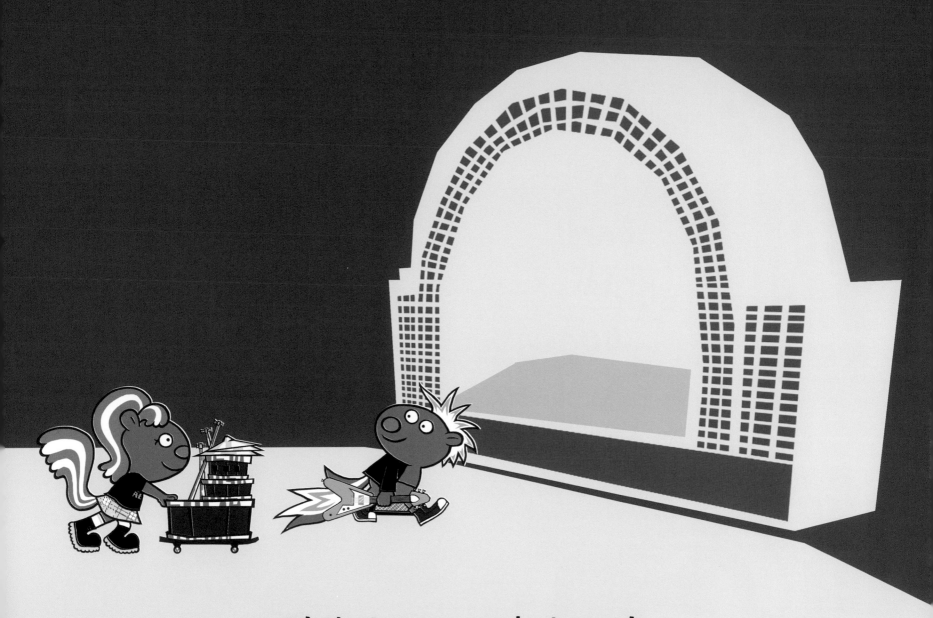

until they were ready to rock.

Together, they sang:

"B-S-F:
YOU'RE THE BEST!
B-S-F:
NEVER LESS!
B-S-F:
PASSED THE TEST!
YOU'RE MY B-S-F!"

"Dig it!" Kit said.

"Rock on," Buzz said.